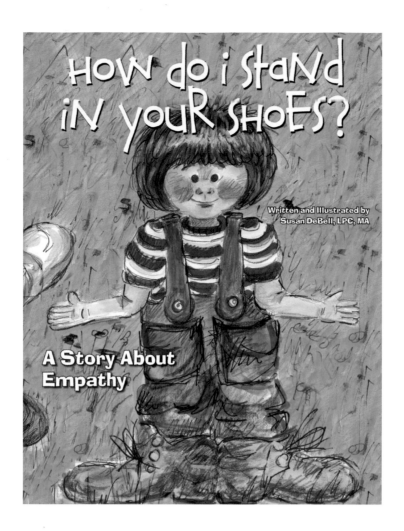

HOW do i StaNd iN YouR ShoES?

Written and Illustrated by
Susan DeBell, LPC, MA

A Story About Empathy

youth light inc.

© 2015 by
YouthLight, Inc.
Chapin, SC 29036
www.youthlight.com

Project Layout by Amy Rule
Project Editing by Susan Bowman

ISBN 978-1-59850-186-5

Library of Congress
2005938410

Printed in China
10 9 8 7 6 5 4 3 2 1

Dedication

"Dedicated to my family, friends, colleagues, students, and everyone that has taught me to *stand in someone else's shoes.*"

Acknowledgement

With special thanks and in memory of Elaine D. Solomon, my friend and mentor whose encouragement and inspiration assisted me in writing this book.

Miranda Peabody was six years old and very smart.

She could spell her
name backwards
and forwards.

She could whistle many catchy tunes.

She could even
stand on one
foot...

chew
sugarless
gum...

and twirl her
short brown hair all at the same time.

She had a mom who was a high school health teacher and a dad who worked in a very large office building.

They both thought Miranda was the best and told her so quite often.

Yes, Miranda was a very smart and talented person, but she had one problem...

She couldn't understand any of the students in her class and she had no patience with them!

In fact, she often got very angry with her classmates and made fun of them. She even called them names!

So every day at school Miranda would remark to her teacher Ms. Klemp that she just couldn't understand anyone in her class and asked her teacher why the other students weren't as smart and talented as she.

She couldn't understand why Thomas Kulpowski couldn't sing the school song on key. Miranda called him "crackle voice" right to his face!

She couldn't understand why Arlene Lee couldn't draw straight lines. Miranda told Arlene that her pictures were the worst ones she had ever seen.

And she couldn't understand why Brian Peters couldn't even finish his homework on time.

Miranda told him he was "slow" and that he better "speed up" if he wanted to be successful in school!

In fact, she couldn't even understand why her teacher, Ms. Klemp would constantly tell her that she should stop losing her temper, making people feel sad, and calling them names. Ms. Klemp suggested that Miranda try to understand other people by "standing in their shoes."

Miranda wondered what standing in someone else's shoes meant, so she decided to ask her best friend, Patricia Greentree, if she knew.

She didn't know what this meant either and neither did Mrs. Dollyrimple, Miranda's favorite doll who just looked at Miranda and smiled.

When she tried to stand in her baby shoes,
they would only fit on the tops of her toes!

Miranda tried on each pair in her carefully sorted pile...

but none of them fit comfortably.

She then remembered a time in art class when she couldn't draw a face no matter how hard she tried.

Then she tried to imagine herself standing in Arlene Lee's fancy pink tennis shoes, trying to draw enough straight lines to make a house.

"How frustrated and sad Arlene must have felt," Miranda thought.

Then she thought of the time she was trying to understand her spelling homework while her father practiced his favorite song over and over again on the saxaphone!

She then imagined herself standing in Brian Peters' black boots trying to finish homework while his brothers ran around screaming.

How sad and embarrassed he must have felt when he had no homework to turn in the next day!

Miranda even imagined herself standing
in Ms. Klemp's high-heeled loafers and
how frustrating it must be to hear
Miranda's name-calling and complaints
about the other students.

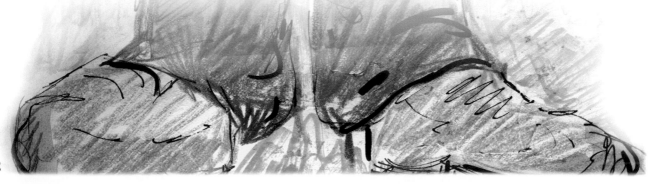

When she had imagined herself in the place of everyone in her class...

Miranda thanked Mrs. Fishpond for her help and ran home to tell her parents what she learned about empathy.

Both of her parents hugged Miranda and told her she really was the best "shoe-stander" (in all of Mountain Stream Elementary School, that is)!!!

When Miranda arrived at school the next day, she looked around at all of her classmates and remembered what it was really like to "stand in their shoes."

In fact, the more "shoe-standing" she imagined...

the more she finally understood what it meant to have empathy and how important it was to understand other people and to be kind to them.

Having empathy was an important tool that Miranda knew she needed to use everyday, everywhere she went, and with everyone she met.

That night Miranda had a wonderful dream that she was standing in the shoes of everyone in the whole world and that she had empathy for them all!

youth light inc.

Social, Emotional and
Learning Skills for Youth

www.youthlight.com

Other Resources Featuring MiRaNda pEabody (& friends)

Written and Illustrated by Susan DeBell

What Should MiRaNda do?
-- Card Game --

Help Miranda solve problems
using important social skills

ISBN: 1598500996

A Story About Bullies,
Bystanders and Friendship

ISBN: 1598500538

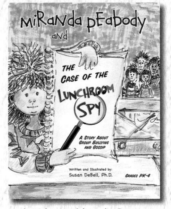

A Story About Group
Bullying and Gossip

ISBN: 1598500627

A Story About Changing
Bullying Behavior

ISBN: 1598501364

A Story of How to Deal
with Worry and Stress

ISBN: 1598500813

A Story About Making
Friends

ISBN: 1598500635

How do i stand iN youR shoEs?

Activity Guide
& Interactive Lessons

Visit www.youthlight.com
for more information.

-- COMING SOON --

P.O. Box 115 • Chapin, SC 29036 • PHONE: 803.345.1070 • FAX: 803.345.0888 • www.youthlight.com